MW01005609

# In Search Of a Hero

**Greg discovers being a hero isn't as easy as it seems.**

## G. Mark LaFrancis

Published By

# M&M

Book Publishing Co.
Natchez, Mississippi
www.inspiringauthor.com
Facebook: Stairway to Reading

**Cover by Aimee Guido**
**Natchez, Mississippi**

# Words to the Wise

While you read "In Search of a Hero," you may notice some words that are not familiar to you. Here is a list of some of them. If you have a dictionary, you may want to keep it handy so you can understand the story better. These words are listed in the order in which they appear in the story.

Page 10: artificial resuscitation
Page 10: revived
Page 11: maneuvered
Page 11: unison
Page 11 commotion
Page 12: embarked
Page 13: feat
Page 14: menacing
Page 14: vicinity
Page 15: nuisance
Page 16: douse
Page 17: fulfill
Page 18: suspicious
Page 19: squandered
Page 21: wafting
Page 22: Heimlich Maneuver
Page 22: suffocate
Page 24: valor

Recommended for readers ages 7-10

# Stairway to Reading™

This book is one of the publications in the Stairway to Reading™ project.

Learn more at:
www.inspiringauthor.org
Facebook: Stairway to Reading
Giving Youngsters the Confidence to Read

# For a Good Cause

A portion of the proceeds will be contributed to The Children's Miracle Network Hospitals, a network of hospitals helping children, including the Blair Batson Children's Hospital in Jackson, Mississippi.

Learn more at:
www.childrensmiraclenetworkhospitals.org

# About the Story

This story was written prior to September 11, 2001, the day that tragedy and terror hurt our beloved country, and thousands of people lost their lives.

On that terrible day, something happened to one special group of people: firefighters, many of whom lost their lives trying to save other people's lives. We gained a new and deserved respect for our firefighters ... and all those who put themselves in danger for us.

In this story, Firefighter Joe is typical of the hundreds of thousands of firefighters who stand ready 24 hours a day, seven days a week, 365 days a year. Firefighter Joe saves a young girl's life and thus inspires nine-year-old Greg to try to become a hero, too.

## 'Makes every firefighter proud'

" 'In Search of a Hero' makes every firefighter proud of his or her profession. ... Although entertaining, this book conveys a positive influence and admiration for all firefighters. It also teaches that anyone, no matter how young or old we are, with just a small amount of training, can save a life or make a difference in another person's life."

-- *Gary Winborne*
*Retired Fire Chief*

IN SEARCH OF A HERO

# Table of Contents

# IN SEARCH OF A HERO

# The Big Story

Newspapers never interested Greg.

He was always too busy.

Too busy playing fetch with his dog, Molly.

Too busy playing Nintendo with his buddy, Mark.

Too busy with soccer, baseball, basketball, whatever sport he could play ...

But newspapers.

Forget it.

That meant sitting down and reading words ... long words ... and many of them.

But one Saturday morning Greg walked to the end of the driveway at his Natchez, Mississippi, home, picked up the newspaper and ... for some reason he still can't explain ... opened it to the front page.

There was a photograph of a firefighter cradling a child in his arms ... a girl of two whom the fireman had just taken from a smoking, flaming building, which appeared in the background in the photograph.

"HERO SAVES BABY GIRL," read the headline.

Greg, whose only interest in the newspaper until then had been reading about the local sports coverage, actually read the whole story about the firefighter before walking in the front door.

*"A city firefighter became a hero Friday when he*

*saved the life of a two-year-old child who became trapped in an apartment fire.*

*"Firefighter Joe Garrison arrived at the scene of the blaze at the Riverbend Apartments shortly after 9 a.m. He was among the first firefighters on the scene.*

*"A woman at a third-story window was screaming, 'Save my baby, save my baby,' according to police reports.*

*"The unidentified woman held an infant in her outstretched arms, preparing to let the child go.*

*"Garrison ran to the building, held out his hands and caught the child just moments after the woman let the girl go.*

*"He then gave the baby, which had stopped breathing, artificial resuscitation.*

*"Moments passed, but Garrison never gave up. Suddenly, when the baby started wailing, everyone knew that Garrison had revived the child.*

*"Fire Chief Gerry Walburn said, 'The crowd started yelling, 'Look, she's saved ... she's saved!'*

*"Walburn said, 'What a hero! We're all proud of Joe.'"*

When Greg read those words, he became overwhelmed.

"WOW!" he yelled.

He yelled "WOW!" again as he ran back into the house. "Shhhhh," said his mom, with her finger over her mouth. "You'll wake your dad and brother."

"But Mom ..." Greg said.

"No 'But Mom' me," she said. "Be QUIET!"

Greg maneuvered in front of her and opened the newspaper's front page.

"That was a very courageous thing," said Greg's mother. "I wonder if he'll get a medal."

"You bet he will," said Greg. "Cool. Way cool. Way cool. Way, way cool."

All through breakfast, Greg stared at the front page photograph and read the story aloud over and over, even to the point of being somewhat annoying. By then his father and brother were up because of all the commotion.

"GREGGG! Stop reading," they ordered in unison.

Although Greg's mouth was silenced, his mind was a symphony of thoughts.

Uppermost in his mind was how he, too, could be like Firefighter Joe and save a life.

That day, and in the days to come, Greg shared his feelings with his family.

"Ya know," he said. "I always thought I was born to do something great.

"I kept thinkin' it was to kick three goals in one soccer game ... or to score three touchdowns in one football game ... or to hit three home runs in a baseball game, or ..."

"GREGGGG!" his family said.

"Ya know," he said. "I think I gotta save a life like Firefighter Joe did."

"Oh, brother," his brother said.

"That's nice," his parents said.

# The Mission

In a few days, Greg, with his new mission in life ... one he declared was created for him ... embarked on a plan.

He decided that to save a life, a life must be in danger.

And that if a life was in danger, he must be aware of the signs, like Firefighter Joe was when he heard the mother's screams.

And that he must be the first to arrive to save the life.

"If that's all there is to this life-saving ... I'll get the job done before I'm ten."

Greg was nine at the time, and he always did everything fast. Very little in Greg's life lasted more than ten minutes, except for when he went to the movies or played a video game or had to sit through a class at school.

But except for those things, Greg flew almost nonstop through life.

"Now stop right there young man," his mother constantly said. "Aren't you forgetting something."

And because Greg was ALWAYS forgetting things, he often forgot what he forgot.

However, Greg did not forget something very important: his mission to save a life. To help him remember, he cut out the story and photograph about

Firefighter Joe and taped it to his bedroom door.

Greg soon realized that lifesaving wasn't as easy - or as quick - as he particularly liked.

As he rode his bicycle through the neighborhood, Greg didn't see one life in jeopardy ... at least not the kind that would qualify him as hero.

Oh, yeah, he helped a toad or two across the road to prevent them from being squished by the neighborhood cars.

And he put the neighbor's old dog Skip back in the fence. He put a bird's nest back up in the crook of a tree, and knocked on Miss Ellie's door when he realized she hadn't come out to get her morning paper by seven a.m.

None of those deeds, though, compared even remotely to Firefighter Joe's feat.

One morning, Greg sat at the breakfast table and let out a heavy sigh.

"Ya know, there must be hundreds of people in our neighborhood. You'd think at least one of them would need help ... even two or three," Greg said. "I just don't seem to be in the right place at the right time."

"Oh, now Greg, don't give up," his mom said, trying to cheer him up.

"Yeah, Greg, maybe a woodpecker will get his beak stuck in a telephone pole," said Greg's twelve-year-old brother Jason, howling with laughter.

"Or maybe little Julie Anne next door will lose the head off one of her Barbies.

"Or maybe the neighbor's cat will gag trying to cough up a furball."

Jason fell on the floor, laughing.

"Stop that," Greg's mother said.

"Thanks, Mom," Greg said.

One afternoon, though, as Greg was riding his bicycle through the neighborhood, he spotted smoke - big clouds of grey, menacing smoke - flowing from the back of a house.

"Oh, no, a fire!" Greg thought, remembering the photograph of Firefighter Joe and the smoke and flames behind him.

"This is my moment," Greg thought, his heart pounding as he sped his bicycle to the house.

He jumped off his bicycle and ran to the side of the house. He couldn't see over the high, barnboard fence.

"Hello!" he hollered. "Are you all right in there?"

No answer.

"HEY!" he yelled again, this time hearing music coming from the house. "Gosh," he thought. "No wonder they can't hear me; the music is too loud. I betcha they don't even know their house is on fire."

Greg, certain this was his moment ... even before he turned ten no less ... looked around.

"Ah ha!" he exclaimed, looking at a garden hose.

He grabbed the hose and unreeled as much as he could.

He turned on the faucet and pointed the hose in the vicinity of the smoke.

The water shot out like a mini-waterfall.

Greg was certain he was saving at least one life ...

maybe two ... maybe three ... maybe a dozen ...

He heard screams.

"Oh, no, I'm too late," Greg thought.

He cranked the faucet all the way.

The screams became even louder.

"HEY! STOP THAT!"

An angry man opened the wooden gate.

He had a spatula in his hand. "Kid, whaddya doin'?" the man asked. "I'm trying to grill up burgers."

Greg peered through the gate to see soaked guests with water-logged buns in their hands.

"Um, um, um ..." was all Greg could get out of his mouth. "Um..."

The man abruptly closed the gate.

As Greg headed home, he heard the man tell his guests, "Some kids really are a nuisance these days."

"A nuisance? A nuisance?" Greg thought. "Try to save a life and that's the thanks you get."

# Maybe This Time

Through the neighborhood grapevine, Greg's family heard what had happened. His father actually laughed when he heard the story.

But, later that night, his father sat him down and said, "Greg, I love you very much. And, maybe you WERE meant to save lives. But the next time make sure there really is a life that needs saving."

"Okay, Dad," Greg said, sounding sad and disappointed.

A couple of days later ... when Greg had forgotten all about trying to douse burgers with a garden hose ... he heard a sound, almost like a cry for help. His ears perked up ... a baby's cry.

He rode his bicycle around the corner, desperately looking right and left. He heard the cries again ... and again.

"I'll find you," he called out to the voice. "I'll find you."

Then, Greg saw a car on the top of a hilly driveway. It began to roll backward toward the street and a deep gully. In the back was a baby in a car seat wailing at the top of her lungs.

No one else appeared to be in the car, which began to pick up speed.

"Gotta do something," thought Greg. "Gotta do something; gotta do something, gotta..."

He spotted a wheelbarrow on the side of the driveway. Greg threw down his bicycle, grabbed the wheelbarrow and gave it a strong push in the path of the car.

"Carunccchh," went the wheelbarrow. "Screeeech, cruncchhh, bannnngggg!"

He indeed brought the car to a grinding halt at the end of the driveway just before it rolled into the street.

What Greg had failed to notice was the driver, who had bent over slightly to roll down the window on the passenger's side to cool off the hot infant.

"Whaddya doin?" the driver yelled.

Again, Greg was speechless. "Uhmmm, uhmmmm."

Greg's dad offered to pay for the busted transmission and brake linings, and to talk with Greg about this hero stuff.

"Now look son," Greg's dad said. "I know you mean well, but you've got to quit this hero thing. It's getting you in trouble and it's costing us money."

"But, Dad ..."

"No 'But, Dad,' Greg, stay out of other people's business."

Greg promised, but only half-heartedly.

Deep inside, he knew he would fulfill his mission.

"I know it will come," he said to himself. "I just know it."

# A Woman in Distress

T hen, one morning as he riding through a remote section of the neighborhood, Greg sensed something wasn't right at mobile home that always appeared a bit suspicious to begin with.

Every time he rode by, the shades were drawn and no one seemed at home even though there was a car in the driveway. He heard that an artist or actress lived there, but no one ever actually saw her.

This time, though, the old car was there along with another, even older car that had rust and bald tires.

Greg peered inside the strange car. It was filled with stuff: coffee cups, candy wrappers, papers and books.

It was filthy from bumper to bumper and side to side. And it had an out-of-state tag on the back ... from up north.

Greg could hear voices from inside the trailer. One voice - a woman's - was high pitched and nervous. The other - a man's - was low and forceful.

"I told you I didn't drive all this way to go home empty handed," the man's voice said.

"And I told you I don't have any money," the woman said.

Greg's mind raced with possibilities.

"What about your family's jewels?" the man asked.

18

"There are no more jewels; my brothers squandered them all on the horse races," the woman said.

"Hah," the man's voice said. "Then I guess I'll take this."

"Oh, no, not my mother's locket. No, not that," the woman said.

Greg's heart pounded with anxiety.

"That poor woman," he thought. He was solidly convinced that this was no mistake. This woman truly needed help.

He raced to the side of the house and found an old baseball bat.

He gulped what seemed to be a grapefruit-sized gulp and ran to the door, pushed it open and leapt into the room, swinging the bat and screaming, "Aiyyyyeeeee!" Greg had seen a lot of Jackie Chan movies and knew that's what he was supposed to yell.

Greg whacked the man in the thigh, smashed a lamp and almost batted a cat off the sofa.

"What the..." the man said.

Greg hollered to the man, "Get back, leave her locket alone!"

Just then, the woman broke out into a laugh. The man did, too.

"We were rehearsing a scene from a play, that's all," the woman said. "This is our director; he came from New York for our performance."

"Oh, no," Greg said. "Not again … I'm gonna be grounded for a year."

Again, the neighborhood grapevine wound its way

back to Greg's home.

The vine became more twisted and winding catching Greg in a web of misplaced desire from which no one it seemed could free him.

This time Greg's father insisted he stop this lifesaving business or risk being grounded ... "FOR A WHOLE MONTH!"

Greg agreed, but not without feeling as though he was giving up ... something he was convinced Firefighter Joe would not do.

# A Proud Moment

$A$ week .. even two ... rolled by with nothing out of the ordinary happening. Greg played ball, swam, walked Molly, pestered his older brother and did all those things a boy is supposed to do in the summer ... all those things except, in Greg's case, save a life.

His parents were happy and the neighbors were happy that they didn't have to worry about being hosed down, or about having their cars damaged or their lamps smashed.

But Greg was unhappy as unhappy could be.

Yet, as school and his birthday approached, he slowly began to forget his glum feelings. "After all," his dad reassured him, "Even if you didn't save a life, you at least tried."

Greg even took the news clipping of Firefighter Joe off his door and put it in his scrapbook on his bookshelf.

"Hey, guys," his dad said one night. "Greg turns ten next week; let's go out to eat."

"Yeah," everyone said.

"Let's try that new place, Sam's Steak House," his dad said.

They arrived to find a packed restaurant with smells of grilled steak wafting through the room. Peanut shells crunched under their feet - a Sam's trademark - and music filled the air.

"This is great," Greg said. "Oh, look, Dad, there's a video game room. Can we play while we wait? Puhleeeeese?"

"Oh, okay," Greg's dad said, giving Greg and his brother two dollars each.

Greg's parents waited in the lounge.

As Greg and his brother walked to the game room, Greg spotted a man holding his throat and waving to the dinner guests at his table.

"Look ...." Greg said to his brother. "That guy's in trouble."

"Don't you ever learn," Greg's brother said. "He's okay, just acting a little goofy. Remember what Dad said?"

Greg ignored Jason and darted around the tables to the white-haired man who began turning blue.

The table guests didn't seem to know what to do.

But Greg had learned from Scout Camp earlier that summer about the Heimlich Maneuver, a process to free a blocked airway.

Greg wrapped his arms around the seated man, clasped his hands together and found just the right spot.

Greg then pulled hard and up.

A piece of steak became dislodged, and the man began to cough, then breathe.

"Oh, son, I don't know how to thank you. I thought I was going to suffocate. What's your name, son?"

"Greg," Greg said.

"Well, Greg, you just saved my life."

People around the table and at tables nearby began to

clap.

The man's wife grabbed Greg's hand and pulled him gently toward her, giving Greg a big kiss on the cheek Greg, turning a little pink in the cheeks, grinned broadly.

She gave Greg a big hug saying, "You know, Greg, I've been married to this man for fifty-five years and I didn't want to lose him, but I didn't know what to do. Thank you, dear boy. Now what can I do for you."

Greg thought and said, "Just don't tell my dad. I'm not supposed to be doing this stuff anymore."

"It's too late, Greg," his dad said looking down at his son with pride.

"You really did save a life," Greg's dad said.

"Yeah," Greg said. "And before my tenth birthday"

That evening, the newspaper reporter came to Greg's home to talk with Greg and take his photograph.

Of course, Greg didn't tell the reporter about the barbecue, the rolling car, or the actress and her director. Instead, he kept saying how he saw the story about Firefighter Joe and how he knew that someday he, too, would save a life.

The newspaper story about Greg's experience was on the front page the next morning with a photograph of Greg holding up the story and picture about Firefighter Joe.

It was Greg's proudest moment, but not the one that he will remember the most that summer.

# The Visit

That night, the doorbell rang, and Greg's mom answered.

"Greg ... someone's here to see you."

Greg ran from the kitchen to the front door.

There was Firefighter Joe in full firefighter's uniform, just as he was in the photograph on the front page. Mayor Smith was there, too, along with several other people in suits.

Greg was speechless.

Mayor Smith stepped up to Greg.

"Young man, we're all proud of you," the mayor said. "Please accept this certificate on behalf of the city."

Greg held out his hand and there was the pretty document with a gold seal in the lower right hand corner.

"For valor and courage," the certificate's words said.

Then, Firefighter Joe came forward.

"Greg," Firefighter Joe said. "I was emotionally moved by your story in this morning's newspaper."

Greg still couldn't speak.

"When I saved that baby, it was the greatest feeling of my life. The city gave me a medal of valor. That was the proudest moment of my life ... until I read that I inspired you. You made me proud, young man. So proud, in fact, that I want to give my medal to you."

Firefighter Joe opened his hand to reveal the shimmering medal hanging from the red, white and blue silk band. He hung it around Greg's neck, gave the medal a gentle pat, and said, "You are proof that even a nine-year-old can be a hero."

Greg looked down at the medal.

Then he looked at Firefighter Joe's face.

In his eyes, Greg could see something that was hard to explain, but something that made Greg feel special and important.

"Thh .. thhhh ... thank you," Greg said.

"No, thank you," Firefighter Joe said.

# IN SEARCH OF A HERO

# About the Author

G. Mark LaFrancis has been a writer for more than twenty-five years, mostly in journalism. He has won many local, state and national writing awards as a reporter and columnist. He is a retiree of the Armed Forces, which he served for twenty-three years in the Air Force, Air National Guard and Air Force Reserve. During his years of service, he earned two Air Force Commendation Medals.

He has been a Boy Scout leader, a youth group leader, and mentor to young writers.

Learn more at:
www.inspiringauthor.org

IN SEARCH OF A HERO